ABOUT THE BANK STREET READY-TO-READ SERIES

Seventy years of educational research and innovative teaching have given the Bank Street College of Education the reputation as America's most trusted name in early childhood education.

Because no two children are exactly alike in their development, we have designed the *Bank Street Ready-to-Read* series in three levels to accommodate the individual stages of reading readiness of children ages four through eight.

○ *Level 1:* GETTING READY TO READ—read-alouds for children who are taking their first steps toward reading.

● *Level 2:* READING TOGETHER—for children who are just beginning to read by themselves but may need a little help.

○ *Level 3:* I CAN READ IT MYSELF—for children who can read independently.

Our three levels make it easy to select the books most appropriate for a child's development and enable him or her to grow with the series step by step. The *Bank Street Ready-to-Read* books also overlap and reinforce each other, further encouraging the reading process.

We feel that making reading fun and enjoyable is the single most important thing that you can do to help children become good readers. And we hope you'll be a part of Bank Street's long tradition of learning through sharing.

The Bank Street College of Education

To Cheré and Roy
—J.O.

To my cats, Paddy and John,
who were my technical advisors
on this book
—C.N.

DO YOU LIKE CATS?

A Bantam Little Rooster Book/February 1993

Little Rooster is a trademark of Bantam Books,
a division of Bantam Doubleday Dell Publishing Group, Inc.

Series graphic design by Alex Jay/Studio J

Special thanks to James A. Levine, Betsy Gould,
Diane Arico, and Ron Puhalski.

Library of Congress Cataloging-in-Publication Data

Oppenheim, Joanne.
Do you like cats?/by Joanne Oppenheim;
illustrated by Carol Newsom.
p.   cm.—(Bank Street ready-to-read)
"A Byron Preiss book."
"A Bantam little rooster book."
Summary: Simple rhyming text and illustrations
present different kinds of cats and their behavior.
ISBN 0-553-09116-6—ISBN 0-553-37107-X (pbk.)
[1. Cats—Fiction.   2. Stories in rhyme.]
I. Newsom, Carol, ill.   II. Title.   III. Series.
PZ8.3.O615Dm   1993
[E]—dc20
92-14113   CIP   AC

Published simultaneously in the United States and Canada

PRINTED IN THE UNITED STATES OF AMERICA

0 9 8 7 6 5 4 3 2

Do You Like Cats?

by Joanne Oppenheim
Illustrated by Carol Newsom

A Byron Preiss Book

A BANTAM LITTLE ROOSTER BOOK

NEW YORK · TORONTO · LONDON · SYDNEY · AUCKLAND

Do you like cats—
short-haired sleek cats,
playing-hide-and-seek cats,

slink-around-the-house cats,
pounce-and-catch-a-mouse cats?

Do you like long-haired cats –
cats with bushy tails and tufts,
cats with paws of silky puffs?

Short fur,
long fur—
what kind of cat
do you prefer?

Would you like a tabby cat,
all striped in gray and black?

8

Or would you choose a calico,
with patches on its back?

How about a Siamese,
born as white as snow?

Did you know that Siamese change color as they grow?

Would you pick a tail-less Manx?
A silvery Russian Blue?

A gray Maltese?
A red Burmese?
Is one of these
for you?

Do you like stray cats—
roaming-night-and-day cats,
nameless-on-their-own cats,
haven't-got-a-home cats,
independent lone cats?

Do you like these?

Alley cats, street cats,
scrounging-food-to-eat cats,
living-by-their-wits cats,
landing-on-their-feet cats –

do you like these?

Do you like pet cats —
stay-at-home-and-play cats,
like-to-have-their-way cats,
napping-through-the-day cats?

Give them a name,
give them a dish,
and give them the space
to do as they wish.

Have you ever heard cats—
Meowling "I'm hungry!
Give me a snack!"

Meowing "I'm lonely!
Give me a pat!"

Purring "Hello!
I'm glad
you're back!"

Mewing and asking
"Did you hear that?"

21

Have you ever seen cats—
hissing and screaming
in anger or fright,
flicking their tails
from left to right,

baring their teeth,
ready to bite,
arching their backs
and ready to fight?

And have you seen
how cats stay clean
from head to tail
and in between?

With sandpaper tongues
all pink and rough
they comb their coats
till they're clean enough.

Have you seen the eyes of cats—
some green,
some gold,
some blue?
Some cats have eyes that do not match,
but most have pairs that do.

Did you know that cats can see
in very little light?
Have you seen their bright eyes glow
like sequins in the night?

Over their eyes,
under their chins,
on the sides of their faces
cats' whiskers grow in.
Wiry whiskers
sprout from their snouts
like extra paws
for feeling about.

And did you know
cats aim their ears
to listen for a sound?
And cats can hear
tiptoeing feet
that barely touch the ground.

Country cats, city cats,
pretty little kitty cats,
cats inside of houses,
cats inside of stores,
sitting on the windowsill
looking out of doors.

Cats in the barnyard,
cats up a tree,
so many kinds of cats
for you . . .

—but not for me!
I don't want a kitten!
I don't want a cat!
I prefer a puppy—
and that's the end of that!